NOTHING FITS A
DINOSAUR

For the Mommasauruses and Daddysauruses

who kept us from extinction

SIMON SPOTLIGHT
An imprint of Simon & Schuster Children's Publishing Division
1230 Avenue of the Americas, New York, New York 10020
This Simon Spotlight edition August 2021
Text and illustrations copyright © 2021 by Jonathan Fenske
SIMON SPOTLIGHT, READY-TO-READ, and colophon are registered
trademarks of Simon & Schuster, Inc.
For information about special discounts for bulk purchases, please contact
Simon & Schuster Special Sales at 1-866-506-1949
or business@simonandschuster.com.
Manufactured in the United States of America 0222 LAK
2 4 6 8 10 9 7 5 3
Library of Congress Cataloging-in-Publication Data
Names: Fenske, Jonathan, author, illustrator.
Title: Nothing fits a dinosaur / by Jonathan Fenske.
Description: Simon Spotlight edition. | New York: Simon Spotlight, 2021. |
Series: Ready-to-reads. Level 1 | Audience: Ages 4–6.
Summary: After being told no drama and to put on his pajamas, the dinosaur is
unimpressed and romps around the house undressed since human clothes are
much too small for such a mighty dinosaur.
Identifiers: LCCN 2021003394 | ISBN 9781665900652 (hardcover) | ISBN 9781665900645
(paperback) | ISBN 9781665900669 (ebook)
Subjects: CYAC: Stories in rhyme. | Clothing and dress—Fiction. | Dinosaurs—Fiction. |
Bedtime—Fiction. | Humorous stories.
Classification: LCC PZ8.3.F3664 No 2021 | DDC [E]—dc23
LC record available at https://lccn.loc.gov/2021003394

NOTHING FITS A
DINOSAUR

BY JONATHAN FENSKE

Ready-to-Read

Simon Spotlight

New York   London   Toronto   Sydney   New Delhi

"No more playtime,"
says my momma.

"Take a bath.
Put on pajamas.

And please, tonight,
no dino drama."

The bath is fun!
I romp and stomp

inside my tiny
bathroom swamp.

But finding jammies
is a chore
when nothing fits a dinosaur!

These claws would tear
a shirt in two.

This cozy quilt
will have to do.

And pants cannot
contain these thighs.

Two sleeping bags
are more my size.

What kind of socks
will warm these toes?

Some pillowcases,
I suppose!

Why stop there?
My feet could use
a decent pair
of stomping
shoes!

But these
will barely fit a mouse!

So let these buckets
shake the house!

And now my noggin
needs a hat.

A lampshade will take care of that.

Did I forget

my underwear?

I have a tail.

I hang it there.

Now I am such
a silly sight.

A dressed-up dino
is not right.

These clothes shall feel
my DINO-MIGHT!

I shed them with
a mega-roar!

I kick them all
across the floor!

No shirt.

No pants.

No socks.

No shoes.

No hat.

No underwear.

I choose
to dress in NOTHING!

Look at me!
NOTHING fits me
perfectly.

Watch me romp

 and stomp

 and roar!

A naked,
happy
dinosaur!

I run wild,
and I run free!

As bare as dinosaurs

should be . . .

. . . till Mommasaurus
roars at me:

nents and Music

Brass

Daniel Nunn

Heinemann Library
Chicago, Illinois

www.heinemannraintree.com
Visit our website to find out
more information about
Heinemann-Raintree books.

To order:

☎ Phone 888-454-2279

🖳 Visit www.heinemannraintree.com
to browse our catalog and order online.

Edited by Dan Nunn, Rebecca Rissman, and Sian Smith
Designed by Joanna Hinton-Malivoire
Picture research by Mica Brancic
Production by Victoria Fitzgerald
Originated by Capstone Global Library Ltd
Printed and bound in China by Leo Paper Products Ltd

15 14 13 12 11
10 9 8 7 6 5 4 3 2 1

Library of Congress Cataloging-in-Publication Data
Nunn, Daniel.
 Brass / Daniel Nunn.
   p. cm.—(Instruments and music)
 Includes bibliographical references and index.
 ISBN 978-1-4329-5058-3 (hc)—ISBN 978-1-4329-5065-1 (pb)
1. Brass instruments—Juvenile literature. I. Title.
 ML933.N86 2012
 788.9'19—dc22   2010044779

Acknowledgments
We would like to thank the following for permission to reproduce
photographs: Alamy pp.8 (© Lebrecht Music and Arts Photo
Library/Chris Stock), 23 centre (© Lebrecht Music and Arts Photo
Library/Chris Stock), 10 (© imagebroker/Martin Siepmann), 17 (©
Lebrecht Music and Arts Photo Library/Odile Noel); © Capstone
Publishers pp. 21 (Karon Dubke), 22 (Karon Dubke); Getty Images
pp. 13 (Hulton Archive/Frank Pocklington/Stringer), 14 (Robert
Harding World Imagery/Maurice Joseph), 18 (AFP/Narinder
Nanu), 20 (Stone/Tony Page); iStockphoto.com pp. 5 centre left
(© DNY59), 5 top right (© Goktugg), 5 bottom left, 5 bottom
right, 5 top left (© RodrigoBlanco), 9 (© Cagri Oner); Photolibrary
pp. 4 (Radius Images), 7 (age fotostock/Josu Altzelai), 11
(Moodboard), 15 (Dallas & John Heaton), 16 (Japan Travel
Bureau), 19 (Corbis), 23 bottom (age fotostock/Josu Altzelai), 23
top (Tetra Images/Rob Lewine); Shutterstock pp. 6 (© Leon Ritter),
12 (© mountainpix).

Cover photograph of a band of tuba musicians in Macau, China,
reproduced with permission of Getty Images (Lonely Planet
Images/Richard I'Anson). Back cover photograph of a tuba player
reproduced with permission of iStockphoto.com (© Cagri Oner).

We would like to thank Jenny Johnson, Nancy Harris, Dee Reid,
and Diana Bentley for their assistance in the preparation of
this book.

Every effort has been made to contact copyright holders of
material reproduced in this book. Any omissions will be rectified in
subsequent printings if notice is given to the publisher.